Fun STEM Challenges

BUILDING TOUGH TOWERS

by Marne Ventura

PEBBLE
a capstone imprint

Pebble Plus is published by Pebble, an imprint of Capstone.
1710 Roe Crest Drive, North Mankato, Minnesota 56003
www.capstonepub.com

Library of Congress Cataloging-in-Publication data is available on the Library of Congress website.
ISBN: 978-1-9771-1296-5 (library binding)
ISBN: 978-1-9771-1776-2 (paperback)
ISBN: 978-1-9771-1302-3 (ebook pdf)

Summary: Describes why towers are useful as well as how to build and test towers made out of toothpicks and marshmallows.

Image Credits
Photographs by Capstone: Karon Dubke;
Marcy Morin and Sarah Schuette, project production;
Heidi Thompson, art director

Shutterstock: canadastock, 7, jayk67, 5, Monticello, 1

All the rest of the images are credited to: Capstone Studio/Karon Dubke

Editorial Credits
Erika L. Shores, editor; Juliette Peters, designer;
Eric Gohl, media researcher;
Laura Manthe, production specialist

All internet sites appearing in back matter were available and accurate when this book was sent to press.

Capstone thanks Darsa Donelan, Ph.D., assistant professor of physics, Gustavus Adolphus College, St. Peter, MN, for her expertise in reviewing this book.

Printed in China.
2493

Table of Contents

What Is a Tower?

A tower is a tall building.
Many people live or work in
towers called skyscrapers.

Why Build Towers?

In cities, tall buildings use less land than wide ones. Long ago, people in castles had towers so they could look out over their lands.

Make Your Own

What can you use to build a tower?

Try building a tower with toothpicks

and small marshmallows.

What other things can you use?

Connectors join pieces together. You can join toothpicks with marshmallows. Connect squares to make cubes. What else might you use for connectors?

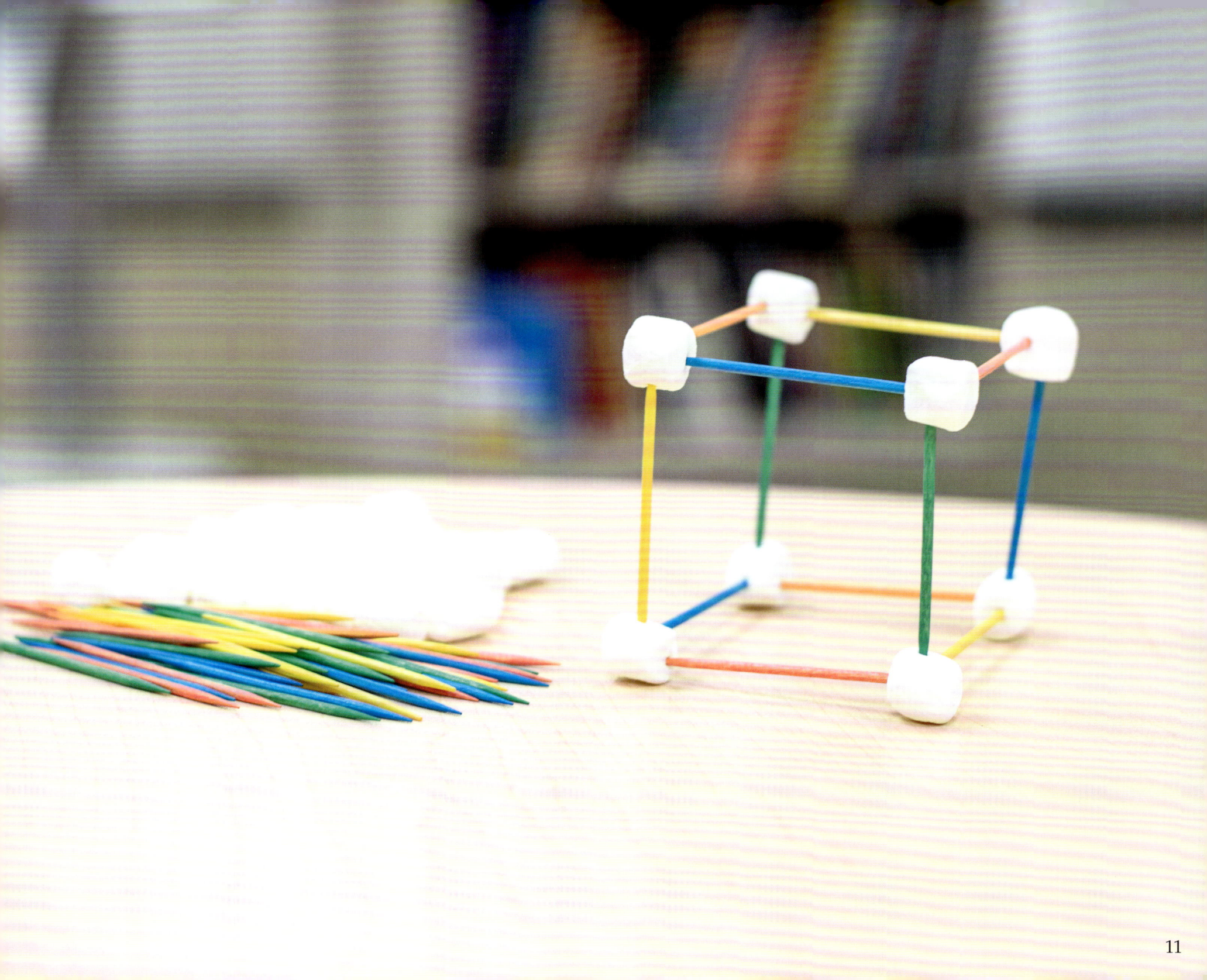

Towers need to be strong.

An X shape makes four triangles.

Triangles are strong shapes.

Add toothpick X's to the walls

of your cube. Is it stronger?

A tall tower can't tip over.

It needs to be stable.

It also needs to hold weight.

Can it hold a flat block or small plate?

Does your tower stand or fall?

The ground around a tower helps it stay up. It is called the foundation. Put salt in a pie plate. Push the bottom of your tower into the salt.

Test It

Ask an adult to help you point a hair dryer or fan at your towers. Do they both move? What can you do to make one of them stronger and more stable?

What Did You Learn?

A tough tower stands up against wind.

Towers need foundations.

Foundations make towers stable.

X shapes make walls stronger.

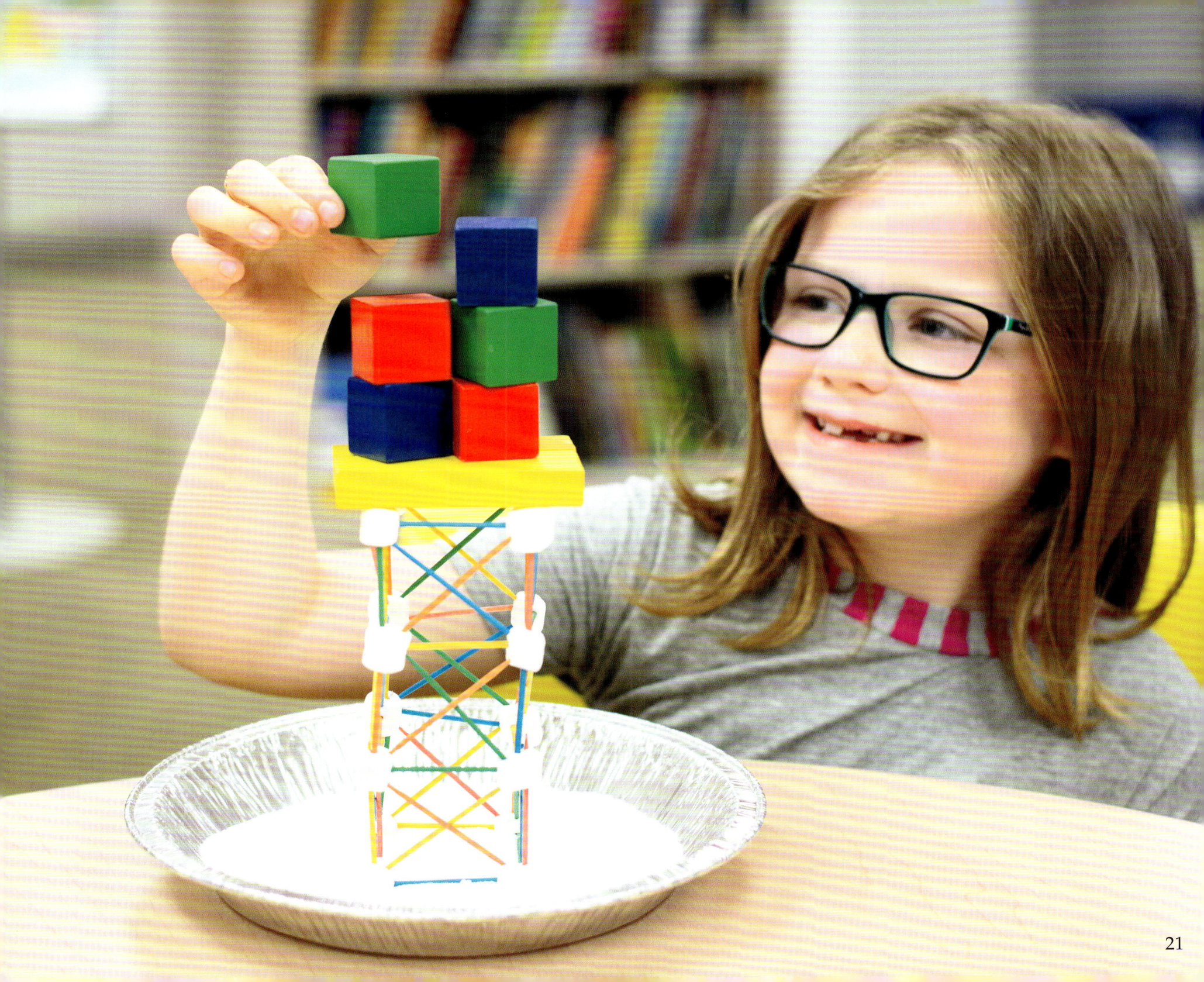

Glossary

connector—a piece that joins two parts

foundation—the base on which something is built

skyscraper—a tall building where people live or work

stable—fixed in place and not easy to tip over

tower—a very tall building

triangle—a shape with three straight sides and three angles

Read More

Bernhardt, Carolyn. *Engineer It! Skyscraper Projects.* Minneapolis: Super Sandcastle, 2018.

Burns, Kylie. *A Skyscraper Reaches Up.* New York: Crabtree Publishing Company, 2017.

Nagelhout, Ryan. *Gareth's Guide to Building a Skyscraper.* New York: Gareth Stevens Publishing, 2019.

Internet Sites

Awesome 8 Skyscrapers
https://kids.nationalgeographic.com/explore/awesome-8-hub/skyscrapers/

Spaghetti Anyone? Building with Pasta
https://www.jpl.nasa.gov/edu/teach/activity/spaghetti-anyone/

Critical Thinking Questions

1. Why do buildings need foundations?

2. Which shapes are used to make towers strong?

3. How can you test a tower for strength?

Index